# Elephant Elephant

## A Book of Opposites

PITTAU & GERVAIS

Harry N. Abrams, Inc., Publishers

# Big

# Small

# Wide

# Narrow

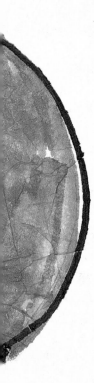

# Start

# Finish

Long

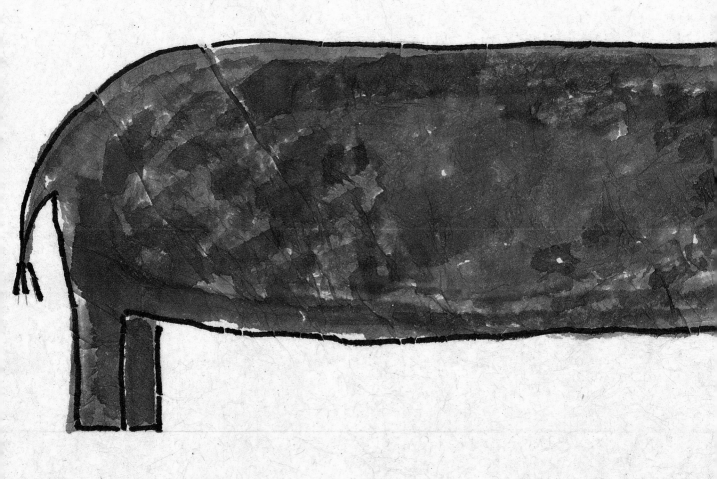

# Top

# Bottom

Back

# Front

# Furry

# Feathered

# Up

# Down

Left

Right

# Angular

# Curvy

# Whole

# Pieces

# Boy

# Girl

# Closed

# Open

# Plains

# Mountains

# Square

# Round

# Uphill

# Downhill

# Plugged

# Unplugged

# Fat

# Thin

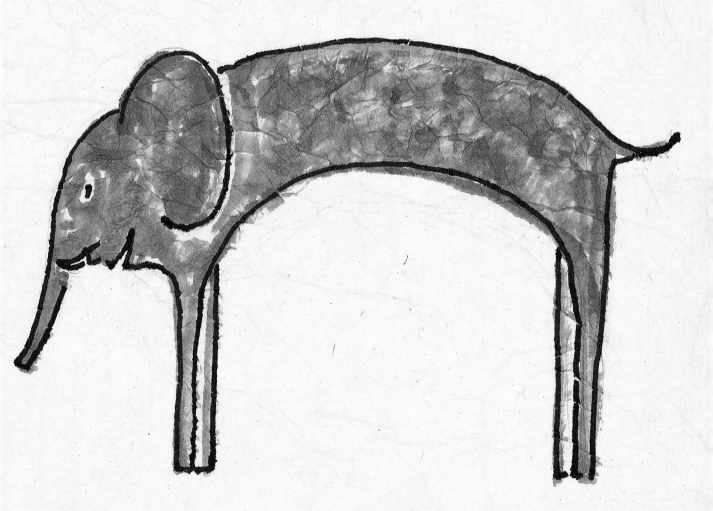

# Hungry

# Full

# Smart

# Stupid

# Inflated

# Deflated

# Subtraction

# Addition

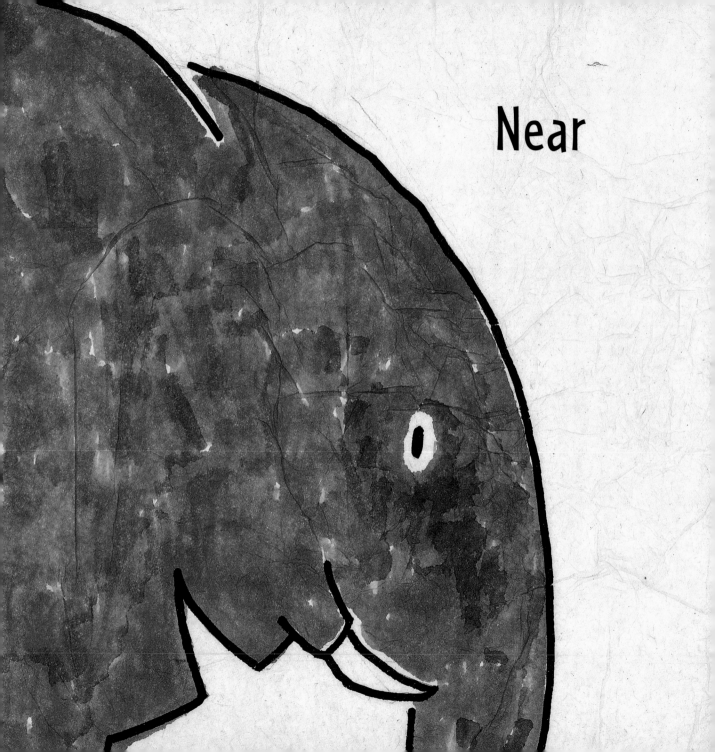

Near

# Far

# Simple

# Complicated

# Broken

# Repaired

# Wrinkled

# Pressed

# Clean

# Dirty

# Solid

# Liquid

# Lit

# Extinguished

# Wrapped

# Unwrapped

# Fluffy

# Spiky

# Visible

# Invisible

# Bright

# Faded

# Torn

# Fixed

# Awake

# Asleep

Designer, English-language edition: Darilyn Lowe Carnes

Library of Congress Cataloging-in-Publication Data
Pittau, Francesco.
[Contraires. English]
Elephant elephant, a book of opposites / Pittau & Gervais.
    p. cm.
ISBN 0-8109-3699-2
1. English language–Synonyms and antonyms–Juvenile literature.
[1. English language–Synonyms and antonyms.] I. Gervais, Bernadette. II. Title.
PE1591.P55 2001
428.1–dc21
2001018854

First published in France under the title *Les Contraires*
Copyright © 1999 Editions du Seuil
English translation copyright © 2001 Harry N. Abrams, Inc.

Printed and bound in China
10 9 8 7 6 5 4

Harry N. Abrams, Inc.
100 Fifth Avenue
New York, N.Y. 10011
www.abramsbooks.com